Copyright © 2000 by Založba Mladinska knjiga, Ljubljana, Slovenia
First published in 2000 under the title *Živalske Uspavanke* by Mladinska, Knjiga,
Ljubljana, Slovenia

English translation copyright © 2006 by North-South Books Inc., New York.

First published in the United States, Great Britain, Canada, Australia, and New Zealand
in 2006 by North-South Books Inc., an imprint of NordSüd Verlag AG, Gossau Zürich,
Switzerland.

Distributed in the United States by North-South Books Inc., New York.

Library of Congress Cataloging-in-Publication Data is available.
A CIP catalogue record for this book is available from The British Library.

ISBN-13: 978-0-7358-2097-5 / ISBN-10: 0-7358-2097-X (trade edition)
10 9 8 7 6 5 4 3 2 1

Printed in Belgium

Animal Lullabies

By Lila Prap

NorthSouth BOOKS

New York / London

Lullaby for Little Owls

Hoooo! Hoooo!

The moon shines
for you.
Night has begun.
Come, little ones,
it's time for fun!

Hooo! Hooo!

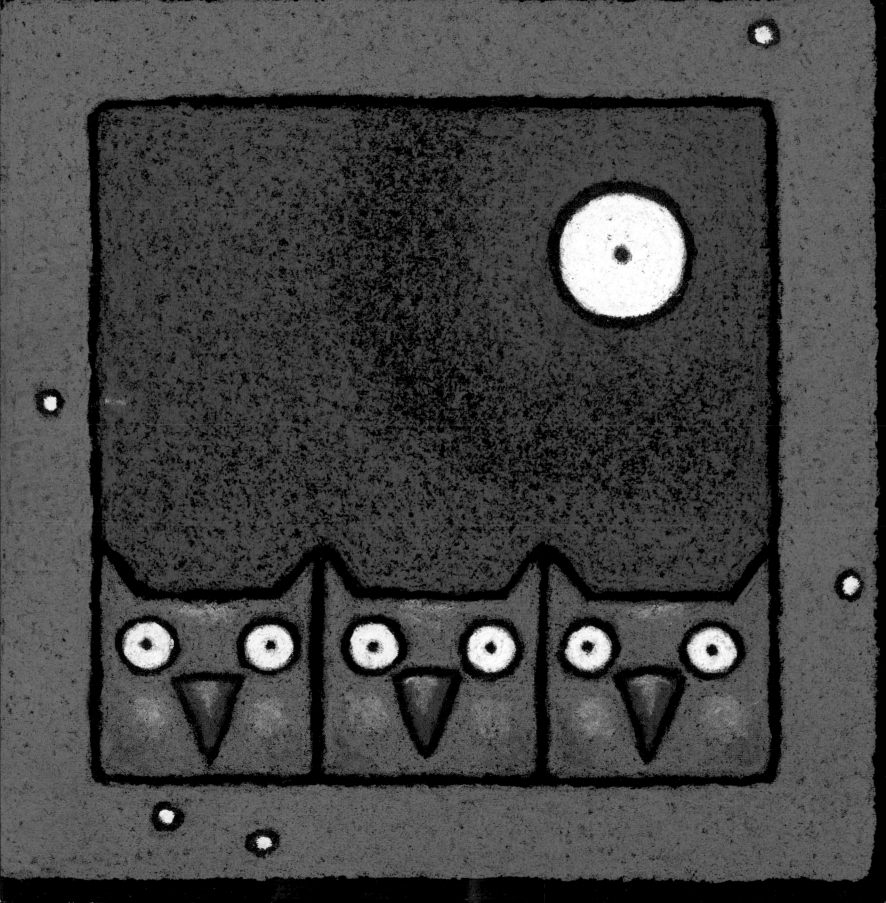

Chick's Lullaby

Time to sleep,
my little peep.
The moon is high
in the evening sky.

Peep, peep, peep, peep,
it's time to sleep.

Sleep, sleep,
peep, peep.

Kitten's Lullaby

Purr, purr,
purr, purr.

Come, my baby,
it's time to sing
a bedtime song
of balls of string.

Purr, purr,
purr, purr.

Slip into dreams
as the moonlight
beams.

Purr, purr,
purr, purr.

Lullaby for Baby Mice

Night by night,
a little bite.

*Nibble, nibble,
nibble, nibble*.

From right to left
and left to right,
until the moon is
out of sight!

Puppy's Lullaby

I'm a good puppy,
and it's time to sleep.
I'll close my eyes and
count some sheep.

I promised Mommy
not to bark,
that I'd be quiet in
the dark.

Oh, but look! There's
the moon!

I'll just sing it a little
bedtime tune.

*Woof, woof, woof,
hooowwwlll!*

Silent Fishy Lullaby

The sleepy fish,
in the water they
splish.

*Pop-pop, pop-pop,
bloop-bloop.*

On the moon they wish,
those sleepy fish.

*Pop-pop, pop-pop,
bloop-bloop.*

Froggy Lullaby

Ribbit, ribbit,
hop, hop.

Night has come,
moonbeams drop
into pond so deep.
Little froggy,
time to sleep.

Ribbit, ribbit,
hop, hop.

Snake's Lullaby

Sssleep, sssleep,
little ssson,
it'sss time to ressst.
The sssilvery moon
coiled in the cloudsss
sssmiles down on
sssleepy snakesss!

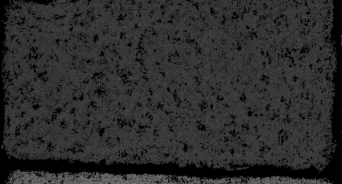

Lullaby for Calves

When the rancher of
the Milky Way is
headed for the skies,
the calf is sleeping
peacefully with
moonlight in her eyes.

Sleepy Sheep

Baaa, baaa, the first
little sheep is sleepy.
On her back she lies—
she's closed her eyes.
Baaa, baaa.

The second little sheep
is sleepy.
Not a peep—
she's sound asleep.
Baaa, baaa.

The third little sheep
is sleepy.
She's asleep it seems—
counting sheep as she
dreams. *Baaa, baaa.*

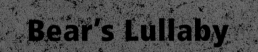

Bear's Lullaby

Sweet dreams, baby bear!
The snow lies on
the ground,
blanketing everything
till spring comes around.

Elephant's Lullaby

Look what happened,
sleepyhead!
No more jumping
on your bed.

Let's fix the bed
and tuck you tight,
sing a song
and say good night.

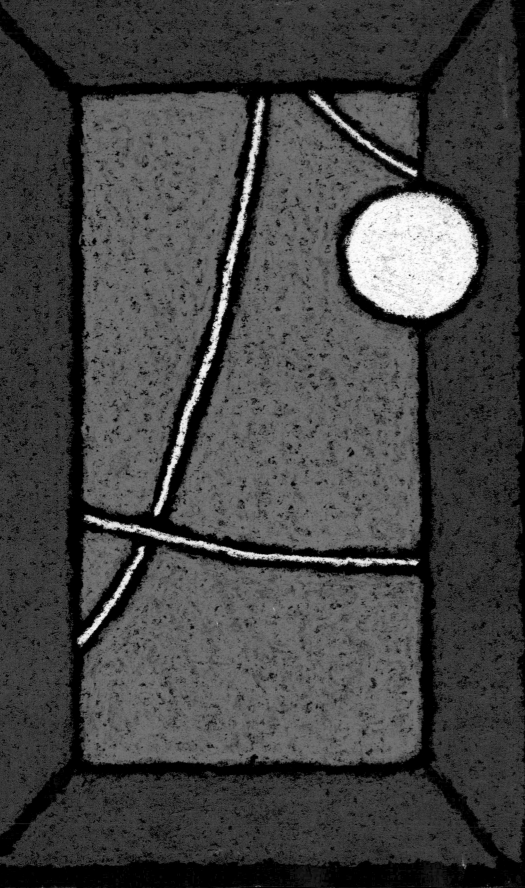

Spidery Lullaby

Good night,
my spiderling.

Here is a bug
to give you a hug,
two crickets to squeak
and kiss your cheek,
and three fat flies
to close your eyes!

Good night,
my spiderling,
good night!

Cricket's Serenade

Chirp, chirp,
chirp, chirp.

Night has come,
the concert's begun.
All crickets in tune
to the light
of the moon.

Chirp, chirp,
chirp, chirp.